This

Welcome to School Book

is especially for

_____

Family Reading Partnership

from

Your School *and the*
Family Reading Partnership
made possible with support from
M&T Bank

Wishing you many hours of family reading
fun and a wonderful kindergarten year!
www.familyreading.org

To Gulliver and Rocket
and to all the little yellow birds
out there . . . especially Auntie Kate,
who was one of the best of them.

Visit us on the Web! www.randomhouse.com/kids

Educators and librarians, for a variety of teaching

tools, visit us at www.randomhouse.com/teachers

Library of Congress Cataloging-in-Publication Data

Hills, Tad.

How Rocket learned to read /

Tad Hills. — 1st ed.   p. cm.

Summary: A little yellow bird teaches Rocket the

dog how to read by first introducing him to the

"wondrous, mighty, gorgeous alphabet."

ISBN 978-0-375-85899-4 (hardcover) —

ISBN 978-0-375-95899-1 (Gibraltar lib. bdg.)

[1. Reading—Fiction.

2. Dogs—Fiction.

3. Birds—Fiction.] I. Title.

PZ7.H563737Ho 2010

[E]—dc22

2008051015

The text of this book is set in Tyrnavia.

The illustrations are rendered in oil paint

and colored pencil.

MANUFACTURED IN CHINA

11

First Edition

Random House Children's Books

supports the First Amendment and

celebrates the right to read.

The author wishes to acknowledge the insight and support of Joan Kindig, associate professor of reading education at James Madison University;
and Jane Morrissey, kindergarten teacher, and Laura Hulbert, lower school learning specialist, both of Brooklyn Friends School.

How Rocket Learned to Read

Tad Hills

schwartz & wade books · new york

Rocket loved to play. He loved to chase leaves and chew sticks. He loved to listen to the birds sing.

Every fall morning, after chasing leaves, Rocket would lie down in his favorite spot under his favorite tree. There he'd sniff the neighborhood smells and settle in for a good nap.

But one day . . . a little yellow bird startled Rocket. "Aha! My first student! Wonderful!" she sang.

Rocket was confused. "Student? I'm not a—"

"But if I am your teacher," the bird interrupted, "then you must be my student."

Rocket found it hard to argue with this bird.

"I am so glad you saw my sign!" the bird chirped.

"Oh, yes, I can *see* it," Rocket said. "But I don't know how to read."

"Can't read? Fantastic!" She waved a wing. "Welcome to my classroom."

"But I just came here to nap," Rocket said.

"No, no! There will be no napping in class," declared the bird. "Except of course during naptime."

"Well then, I can take a nap over here," said Rocket. "I've had a very busy morning."

"Not to worry, I'll be around every day," chirped the bird. "Until the weather turns."

class starts today

As Rocket breathed in the crisp air, the little yellow bird hung her banner. "Ah, the wondrous, mighty, gorgeous alphabet," she marveled. "Where it all begins."

Opening up a book, the bird began to read. She sang out the story of an unlucky dog named Buster who'd lost his favorite bone.

A cool breeze carried her lively voice across
the yard. At first Rocket was disturbed.

But before long he found himself captivated.

To Rocket the story was as delicious as the earthy smells of fall. It was as exciting as chasing leaves. He closed his eyes and listened to every word.

"'As Buster dug and dug under the lilac bush,'" the bird read, "'he felt something familiar.'"

Rocket waited. *Was it the bone?* he wondered.

Silence.

"Was it the bone?" he called to the bird.

More silence.

"WAS IT THE BONE?!"
Rocket hollered.
  Suddenly he was
rushing to the tree.

"WELL,
WAS IT?"

But the little yellow bird was gone.

The next morning Rocket arrived early.

At last the little yellow bird appeared. "Hello! How wonderful to see you in class," she chirped. "I can tell by your waggy tail that you are well rested."

"I'd like to hear the end of the story, please," said Rocket.

"That seems like a fine way to start the day," chirped the bird. She gave Rocket a name tag and began to read.

Every day Rocket
returned to the little yellow
bird's classroom.

In the morning the bird
taught him a new letter,

until he had learned all
of the wondrous, mighty,
gorgeous alphabet.

Together they sang out the sounds that each letter makes and spelled the sounds they heard around them.

With a *G* and many *R*s they spelled Mr. Barker's growl.

GRRRRRRRRRR!

They spelled the sound of the wind, which was growing colder by the day.

WHHOOSS.

HHHHHHH...

Soon they were spelling words, like *F-A-L-L* for the gusty time of year, and *R-E-D* for the color of the leaves.

And each afternoon the bird read a story. She read stories about dogs and birds. She read about leaves changing colors and about birds flying south for the winter.

Then one day the weather turned and the letter banner disappeared.

"See you again in the glorious spring," the bird sang.

And as she flew into the wintry sky, she called, "Don't forget! Words are built one letter at a time!"

The days grew shorter, and
the leaves fell from the trees.

The grass became crunchy.
Soon Rocket's classroom
disappeared under the snow.

He remembered the little yellow
bird's alphabet and practiced his letters.

Rocket thought about the bird's sweet chirp while he
sounded out words

like *D-I-G*

and *W-I-N-D*   and *C-O-L-D.*

He made new friends and spelled their names.

"Hello, *E-M-M-A*."

"Hi there, *F-R-E-D*."

He spelled *everything*.

S-U-N.

M-E-L-T.

When Rocket spelled *M-U-D*, he knew that spring,
as it always does, had returned.

The breeze blew warmer, the grass grew greener, and a sign appeared.

Early the next morning, Rocket rushed to his classroom. As he waited, he spelled *W-A-G*.

Soon the little yellow bird arrived. "Aha! My star student!" she sang. "How wonderful to see you. I can tell by your waggy tail that you are ready for class."

Welcome Back, Rocket

Then together they began to read. They read stories about birds flying north in the spring. They read about picnics in the warm sun. And they read about Buster, the lucky dog who found his bone under the lilac bush.

And when they were done, they read it again.

And again.

And *A-G-A-I-N*.